Royal Magic

by Ruth Chew

A
LITTLE APPLE
PAPERBACK

SCHOLASTIC INC.
New York   Toronto   London   Auckland   Sydney

ISBN 0-590-44742-4

Copyright © 1991 by Ruth Chew.
All rights reserved. Published by Scholastic Inc.
APPLE PAPERBACKS is a registered trademark of Scholastic Inc.

12 11 10 9 8 7 6 5 4 3 2 1   1 2 3 4 5 6/9

Printed in the U.S.A.   40

First Scholastic printing, October 1991

For my grandson,
Zachariah Jared Silver

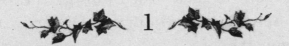 1

"Look at the family of monkeys, kids!" Mr. Edwards said.

Jack read the sign next to the big diorama. "They're chimpanzees, Dad."

Cindy stared through the glass at the jungle scene. "It's like a magic window!"

Mrs. Edwards nodded. "I've never been in this part of the museum before. The place is so very big."

"I got lost here once," Mr. Edwards said. "Maybe that's why they won't let kids in without adults."

Today was George Washington's birthday. They all had a holiday. It was cold and windy. The Edwards' family lived in Brooklyn. They had decided to take the subway to the Museum of Natural History in Manhattan.

There was an entrance right inside the subway station. Mr. Edwards had checked their heavy coats in the museum coatroom. Then they took the elevator to the Hall of Africa.

Now they were in the upstairs gallery of the hall. It was not crowded here. They could stand right in front of the dioramas. Each one had a landscape with a different kind of animal in it.

"Giraffes!" Mrs. Edwards walked over to another diorama.

"I haven't finished looking at the chimps," Cindy told her father.

"Neither have I," Jack said.

"That's okay. Just stay right here so you won't get lost." Mr. Edwards laughed. "I'll bring your mother back as soon as she's seen enough giraffes." He went to join his wife.

"Jack," Cindy said. "Everything in this diorama seems so *real*. Look at the sunlight shining on that river way over there. And the woods seem to go on forever!"

The diorama showed four chimpanzees. One half-grown male chimp was posed as if he were climbing along a tree branch. The mother of the family had broken the top off a tree to make a nest. The big sister was about to eat a pink fruit that grew in clusters near her. A very small chimp had one arm out to grab some of the fruit away from her.

"I can feel a warm breeze," Jack

said. "Maybe they turned up the heat in the museum."

Cindy looked around to see where the breeze was coming from.

It came from the leaves of a grove of trees *behind* her. Jack and Cindy were in a tree in the middle of a thick jungle!

Cindy was frightened, but she wasn't going to let her brother know it. She grabbed hold of a branch. "Jack, look! The little chimp is moving!"

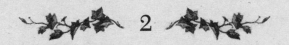

2

JACK was two years older than his sister. "Maybe this is some new computer thing the museum put in to make the dioramas seem alive," he said.

"You don't suppose it's *magic*?" Cindy whispered. She had always longed to have a magical adventure.

"Don't be silly!" Her brother stared at the chimpanzees.

The little chimp had grabbed a piece of fruit. His big sister tickled him. He squeaked with laughter and almost dropped the fruit.

The mother chimpanzee looked up from her nest-building. When she caught sight of Cindy and Jack, she bared her sharp teeth and waved the broken-off treetop at them.

9

"We won't hurt you," Cindy said.

Jack didn't say a word but pulled a bag of M&M's out of the pocket of his jeans. He put four little bright-colored pieces of candy on the branch. Then Jack grabbed Cindy's hand and dragged her closer to the trunk of the tree and away from the chimps.

All four chimpanzees stared at the little round candies gleaming on the mossy branch. The smallest chimp jumped onto the branch, grabbed the candy, and leaped to the safety of his mother's arms.

His mother dropped the broken treetop and held her little one close to her. His brother and sister rushed over to take the candy away from him, but the mother chimpanzee made all three wait while she tasted a piece.

She popped a bright red M&M into her mouth and let the sugar

coating melt. When she tasted the chocolate, she gave a happy grunt and handed each of her children one of the little round candies.

Then the mother chimpanzee picked a cluster of the pink fruit from the tree near her and held it out to Cindy and Jack.

"Come on, Jack, she wants to be friends now." Cindy crawled back along the branch.

The mother chimpanzee patted Cindy's shoulder and popped something that looked like a plum into her mouth.

It was much too sour to be a plum, but Cindy ate it anyway.

Next the chimpanzee waved the bunch of fruit at Jack. He came over to be patted and fed, too.

"Why didn't you warn me, Cindy?" he said. "This stuff is awful!"

His sister grinned. "You know what you can do about it, don't you?"

"What?" Jack asked.

"Complain to the museum about their computer," she told him.

3

BEFORE Jack could answer, there was a crackling sound below. Cindy and Jack and the chimpanzees looked down.

They saw a large animal with twisted horns leap out of the bushes and fall at the foot of the tree. Three men came running after it.

The mother chimpanzee gave a low cry. The little chimp grabbed onto her long black fur. She took hold of a hanging vine and swung herself into the next tree. Her two other children followed. The chimpanzees swung from one tree to another and were soon out of sight in the thick jungle.

Jack and Cindy watched the chimpanzees until they were gone. Then they looked at the ground again.

The big animal lay on its side without moving. The three men sat on the ground nearby. They were shiny with sweat and looked very tired.

One man seemed older than the others. He was tall and strong-looking and was holding a bow and a case of arrows. Now Cindy and Jack saw that an arrow had struck the big animal and killed it.

"Elonmo, what a great hunter you are!" a young man with a spear said.

"Thank you, Uzi," Elonmo said. "If you work hard, lad, you'll learn the trade, too."

The third man was older than Uzi, but not as old as Elonmo. He was slender and not very tall. All three were wearing short wraparound skirts of cotton cloth, but there was a woven pattern on the smaller man's skirt. And he wore shiny brass rings on his arms and legs. "The bongo will make a fine gift to take to the Oba, Elonmo," he told the hunter. "His Majesty likes all kinds of antelope meat."

"It is good of you to tell me that, Atuke," Elonmo said. "I was afraid he'd be disappointed if I didn't trap a leopard."

Atuke pulled a carved ivory flute out of a twist of his skirt and began to play a gentle tune.

The two children could hear every word the men below them said. "Jack," Cindy whispered to her brother. "Do you still think we're in the museum?"

"No," he told her. "But I don't have any idea where we are."

"Those guys seem to know where *they* are," Cindy said. "Let's go down and talk to them."

Jack looked at the three men below them. "We'd better watch out they don't shoot us full of arrows."

Cindy thought for a minute. Then she called as loud as she could. "Atuke!"

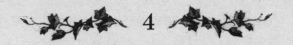

4

At the sound of his name the smallest of the three men looked around. "Who calls me?"

The other men stood up. Uzi picked up his spear, and Elonmo fitted an arrow to his bowstring.

"I'm Cindy," she yelled down to the men under the tree. "And this is my brother Jack. We're stuck up here, and we're lost."

"Cindy may be stuck, but I'm not," Jack said. "She's just not any good at tree climbing."

"You'd better not try any tricks," Uzi warned. "Come out of the tree, and I will help your sister down." He stood beside the tree, holding his spear ready while Jack worked his way to the ground.

Atuke put away his flute and got to his feet. He stared at the brass rivets on Jack's new blue jeans and at his fancy plaid cowboy shirt.

Jack held out his hand.

Atuke bowed and took Jack's hand in both of his. "I will do what I can to help you," he said.

Uzi handed his spear to Elonmo, and then swung himself up into the tree and gently carried Cindy down.

"Thank you." Cindy held out her hand.

Uzi kneeled before her and held out both his hands. She shook them. Then he stood up. "I am honored to serve you."

It seemed to Cindy that the young hunter was looking at the little flowers printed on her dress as if he'd never seen anything like them before.

Then Uzi went down on his knees

to Jack. "Forgive me for my behavior, young sir. I have been taught to watch for enemies in the forest."

Jack held out his hand to him. "You are right to be careful. We're not supposed to talk to strangers, either. But we don't know anyone here."

Uzi took Jack's hand in both of his.

19

Elonmo gave Uzi back his spear. Then he bowed to the two children. He, too, used both hands to shake theirs. "I am Elonmo, chief hunter to His Majesty, the Oba of Edo. This young man is my helper, Uzi. Of course you know who Atuke is."

"No," Cindy told him. "We heard you talking together. Jack was afraid you would shoot us if you saw us before we let you know we were in the tree. I called Atuke's name because I'd heard you say it, and because he was playing the flute."

Atuke's face crinkled into a grin. "And not fingering a bowstring, you mean," he said.

"You will have to get used to Atuke's rude ways, Cindy," Elonmo warned her. "He is the Royal Jester."

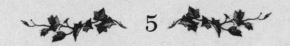

5

"HIS Majesty the Oba gave me a few days off," Atuke said. "I decided to come with my friends on their hunting trip." He smiled at the children. "How did you come here?"

Jack and Cindy told the jester what had happened. The two hunters listened to the story, too. All three men kept looking at the children's clothes.

Atuke asked questions about everything. Cindy had to describe the museum and the dioramas. "And what will Mom and Dad think when they find we're not there?"

The jester listened to her story. At last he said, "It sounds very much like the Oba's palace. But somehow you

21

young people have fallen under a magic spell. Come with us to Edo. Perhaps the learned diviners there will know how to break the spell."

There was a little clearing beneath the tree where the shadows kept the underbrush from growing.

"What's that?" Jack pointed to a large jug at the edge of the clearing.

"Drinking water," Uzi told him. "Are you thirsty?"

Cindy and Jack went over to the jug. On one side of it they saw a flat slab of wood with a few little white seashells on it. Next to the slab was a clamshell.

"Oh, aren't they pretty!" Cindy reached for one of the little shells.

"Stop!" Uzi commanded. "Those cowries have been put here to pay for the water people have drunk."

"Oh," Cindy said. "They're *money*!

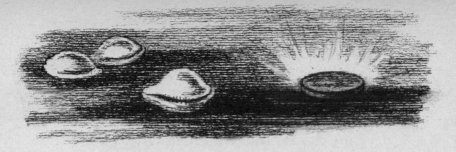

I wouldn't touch money that didn't belong to me." She pulled a shiny new penny out of her pocket and put it on the slab with the cowries. "That's our money."

Uzi smiled. "I know you didn't mean to take the cowry."

Atuke and Elonmo had walked over to join them. They leaned over to look closely at the penny.

"There's a man's head on one side," Elonmo said.

Atuke turned over the coin. "And a palace on the other." He handed the penny back to Cindy, and took five cowry shells from a leather bag slung around his neck. "This will pay for drinks for us all." He picked up the clamshell and carefully poured water from the jug into it. Then he handed the shell to Cindy.

She drank the water slowly, trying not to spill a drop. The water was clear and tasted good.

When Cindy had finished drinking, the jester filled the shell again and gave it to Jack. Then Elonmo and Uzi each had a drink. Finally Atuke poured some for himself.

When they had finished Cindy asked, "Who puts the water there?"

"Someone who lives around here and has a well on his farm," Elonmo told her. "The water in the river is not good to drink."

Uzi took a big curved knife from a leather case that hung from his belt.

"That looks like a pirate's cutlass," Jack whispered to his sister. "I wonder what he's going to do with it."

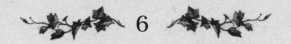

6

Uzi walked over to a young tree. He used the big knife to chop it down. Then he stripped the branches from it and cut off the top. Now he had a long pole.

Elonmo pulled a length of strong string from the pouch at his waist. "We have to tie the bongo to the pole so we can carry it back to the city," he told the children.

Jack and Cindy came over to help. Jack showed Elonmo the square knot he had learned in the Boy Scouts.

The hunter was pleased. "That's a handy trick to know. It's hard to keep the bongo from sliding off the pole."

"If we used two poles we could all carry the load," Cindy said.

"You have a good idea," Atuke told her, "but the forest paths are only wide enough for one person at a time." He rubbed his chin. "Elonmo, let's go along the river. Then we could use Cindy's idea at least part of the way."

"We'll try it," Elonmo said. "Uzi, cut another pole while Jack and I get the bongo firmly tied to this one."

When they were ready to leave the clearing, Elonmo broke several twigs and bent them to point the way they were going to go.

"Why is he doing that?" Cindy asked the jester.

"So he'll know if we're walking in a circle," Atuke told her. "It's easy to get lost in these woods."

Now Cindy noticed a narrow footpath in the underbrush. Elonmo handed her his bow and the case of arrows. "You go first, Cindy," the

hunter said. "You're short enough for me to see over your head. I'll be right behind you to take the bow and arrows if I need them." He picked up one end of the pole that had the bongo tied to it.

Uzi took the other end. Jack came after him, holding Uzi's spear. The jester was last. He carried the second pole the young man had cut.

They started walking single file through the jungle.

The path led through a tangled growth of vines and tall trees growing close together. Cindy saw small green orchids clinging to a tree beside the path. She started to pick one.

"Watch out!" Elonmo cried.

Now Cindy noticed a snake coiled among the flowers! She moved away and tiptoed past.

A little farther on, a lizard with a sky-blue tail ran across the path in front of her.

The forest was full of noises. All around there was the song of insects. Cindy could hear a pair of parakeets arguing over where to build their nest. Then a tribe of monkeys went howling through the trees.

It seemed to Cindy as if they had been walking for hours. At last they stepped out of the forest into the sunlight.

"Here's the river," Elonmo said.

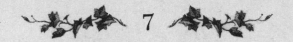

7

Uzi and Elonmo tied the bongo so that it hung between the two poles.

"Give the spear to your sister, Jack," Elonmo said.

Jack handed Cindy the spear.

"Do you think you can carry that as well as the bow and arrows?" Elonmo asked her.

Cindy walked a few steps. "It's heavy, but I can do it."

"Jack," Elonmo said. "Come up front with me. Uzi can go behind you next to Atuke. That way we're balanced."

Jack and the three men picked up the poles and started across the open ground toward the river.

Cindy walked beside Elonmo. "You're right," he told her. "It's much easier to carry the bongo this way."

As they came closer to the water, the ground underfoot began to be marshy. They had to walk around strange trees with wild tangled roots growing out into the air. Tall clumps of reeds blocked their way. The hot sun beat down on Cindy's head. It had been much cooler in the woods.

Soon there were pools of water oozing out of the ground. They were walking through a swamp. Cindy was glad she wasn't wearing new shoes.

With a loud cry a long-necked bird flew out of a patch of marsh grass. Something that looked like a log opened a pointed jaw with jagged teeth and jumped into the air after the bird. "Hey, Cindy," Jack yelled, "did you see that crocodile?"

"Why don't we try to catch him?" Atuke said. "I've heard the Oba say a crocodile is the best offering he can make to his Altar of the Hand."

"Thanks for telling me," Elonmo answered. "Uzi and I will come back by ourselves another time to catch a crocodile. There seem to be quite a lot of them around here. Be careful, Cindy. Stay close to me."

Cindy and Jack looked around. Every pool of water seemed to have bulging eyes looking out of it. And every log looked like a crocodile.

"I guess my idea wasn't so good after all," Cindy said. "I'm sorry I got us in this mess."

"It's my fault, Cindy," Atuke said. "I suggested we go along the river."

Elonmo laughed. "Uzi and I know what the riverbank is like. I just wanted to try the two-pole idea. Now

I think we'd better get away from here before the sun goes down."

They carried the bongo around a bend of the river and then headed back to the forest.

At the edge of the trees was a large clearing with a double stockade of thick logs around it. Along the inside of the stockade Jack and Cindy saw one-story houses with walls made of sun-dried bricks and roofs woven of palm leaves.

Elonmo led them over to a thick wooden door in the stockade and made a sign to Jack and the others to put down the bongo. Then he pounded on the door with both fists.

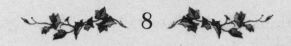

8

ELONMO knocked and knocked, but no one came to the door. The sun was beginning to set.

Atuke took out his flute and began to play a sad sweet tune.

When the jester stopped playing, a deep voice on the other side of the wall demanded, "Who's there?"

"It is I, Elonmo, chief huntsman to His Majesty, the Oba," Elonmo said. "With me are a young prince and princess from a far country as well as the Royal Jester and Uzi, my faithful helper. The prince and princess do not know how to defend themselves against the creatures of the forest. I ask shelter for the night."

There was a rumbling noise. The heavy door swung open.

A stocky man stood in the doorway. When he saw Elonmo he bowed and held out both hands in greeting.

Cindy noticed that Elonmo held out only one hand. The man shook it. "I am Agebeye, the master of this household. It is an honor to welcome the king's huntsman. Please come in."

They carried the bongo into a courtyard that had houses on all sides. Agebeye shut and barred the door again.

Jack and the three men put down the bongo. Then Elonmo introduced Jack, Cindy, Atuke, and Uzi to their host. When Agebeye held out both hands to Jack, Cindy saw her brother start to give both of his in return. She grabbed hold tight of Jack's left hand. He had to shake hands the same way he did at home.

Now it was Cindy's turn. She let

go of Jack's hand and held out her own to Agebeye. He bowed low.

A boy of about Cindy's age walked over to give a carved wooden box to the host.

"This is Itua, my oldest son," the master of the house told them.

Again they went through the shaking hands ceremony. Then Agebeye opened the box and held it out to Elonmo.

Elonmo took a nut out of the box and said a prayer such as many people say before a meal. He broke the nut into small pieces and ate one himself. After that he handed a little piece of the nut to everyone else there.

Now quite a few people started to come out of the houses in the courtyard.

Elonmo broke more nuts and gave a piece to each of them.

"Cindy," Jack said. "What do these taste like?"

"I don't know," Cindy told him. "But I know I've tasted something like them." She grabbed the jester's arm. "Atuke, what are these things?"

"Kola nuts, of course!" Atuke told them.

Jack and Cindy looked at each other. "Of course!" they both said.

The nuts tasted like Coca-Cola!

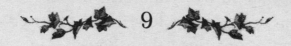 9

WOMEN were walking around carrying
large gourds. Little girls passed out
wooden drinking cups to everybody in
the courtyard. The women filled the
cups from the gourds.

Jack sipped the sweet liquid.
"Yum!" he said. "What is it, Atuke?"

"Palm wine," the jester told him.

"Our parents don't want us to drink
wine," Cindy said.

"Just pretend you're drinking,"
Atuke whispered. He looked around to
see if anyone was near enough to hear
him. "It's rude not to eat and drink
what's given to you, but you

38

must never finish all of it. Remember!"

"There seem to be a lot of things to remember," Jack said. "What's with the handshaking?"

The jester laughed. "I saw Cindy stop you from holding out both your hands to Agebeye."

"What's wrong with that?" Jack asked.

"He's only a farmer. You're a prince," the jester reminded him. "You only have to give both hands to a king."

Jack started to turn red. "Is that why you and Uzi and Elonmo gave Cindy and me both hands?"

Atuke nodded. "Only royalty wears cloth like yours, and only the Oba is permitted to have brass." He pointed to the rivets on Jack's jeans. Then he smiled. "But I soon learned you're not really a prince and princess."

Cindy tried to smooth her hair. "How can you tell?"

"I live in the palace, and I'm around royalty a lot. You don't act like them," Atuke said. "Itua, our host's oldest son, acts more like a prince than Jack does." He spoke very low. "It's important to let people *think* you're important. They can tell you don't belong here. You don't have the tribal

marks on your face." He pointed to the tattoos on his nose and forehead.

Jack looked around the courtyard. "What about the man over there building a fire? He doesn't have the marks. And how about that little girl? She doesn't have them either."

"They're slaves," the jester said. "Slaves and foreigners don't have our tribal marks."

Cindy held her head high and tried to act like a princess. Jack squared his shoulders and stuck out his chin.

"That's better," Atuke said. "Here comes Agebeye with his senior wife and his mother. You must hold out both hands to his mother."

"Why?" Jack wanted to know.

"Because old people are worthy of reverence," Atuke told him.

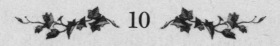 10

CINDY and Jack held out both hands to Agebeye's mother and one to his senior wife. Everybody bowed. Jack and Cindy tried hard to act like royalty.

When Agebeye and the two women had gone, Jack asked Atuke, "What's a senior wife?"

"That means she's the first one Agebeye married," the jester told him. "She teaches the others how to raise their children. They have to obey her."

"In our country men only have one wife at a time," Cindy said.

Atuke laughed. "Our women wouldn't like that. They'd have to do all the work alone. This way they each have an apartment for themselves and their children, but they always have the other wives close by to laugh and talk with. And when they're sick or have a new baby, they help each other."

Through the open doorway of one of the houses Jack and Cindy could see children carrying in wood. They stacked it next to a fire that burned there.

There were no windows in the houses. The roofs were open in the middle to let light in and smoke out. A large iron pot was set over the fire.

"That must be the kitchen," Cindy said.

Several women carried jugs of water from a well in the courtyard to pour into the pot. Then they put in chunks of meat and poultry and a great many yams.

The senior wife was telling the others what to do.

"She looks as if she's directing traffic," Jack whispered to Cindy.

The sun had gone down. It was very dark. A man used a burning stick from the kitchen fire to light the oil lamps hanging in the doorways of the houses.

"He doesn't have tribal marks," Jack said. "Is he a slave?"

Atuke nodded.

Elonmo and Uzi came walking over. They had been talking to Agebeye.

"These people are preparing a feast in our honor," Elonmo said. "We'd better get washed before dinner." He led the way over to the well.

Cindy splashed water on her face and hands and ran her fingers through her hair. There was no need for towels. The warm air dried her almost at once.

When they had all finished washing, Elonmo pointed to a large house next to the kitchen. "That's where the dinner will be served. Let's go and see where we're supposed to sit."

All five of them walked into the dining room. The floor was spread with mats of woven fiber.

Agebeye was seated facing the door, beside his senior wife and their children. "Come and sit by me," he said.

Elonmo led Jack and Cindy to a mat near their host. Atuke and Uzi followed. As soon as they sat down, the room began to fill with people.

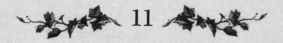

11

THE dining room was lit with oil lamps hanging from the rafters overhead.

Agebeye's mother and her other grown children sat together. Each of Agebeye's wives sat on a different mat with her children.

When everyone was seated, a slave woman brought in a bowl of water. She held the bowl on her knee for Agebeye and the senior wife to wash their hands.

When they had finished, she took away the bowl. Then she helped a man slave carry a large basin of food from the kitchen next door for each mat.

Cindy noticed that the two slaves also put a big basin of food on a mat where the little slave girl was sitting.

When every mat had a basin of food, the man slave closed the wooden door. Then the woman slave passed out pretty mussel shells to be used as spoons.

The two grown-up slaves sat down on the mat beside the little slave girl.

Agebeye dug his mussel shell into his basin of food, and everybody began to eat.

Jack and Cindy scooped their food out of the same basin as Atuke, Elonmo, and Uzi. It was a good-tasting stew, and all five of them were hungry. There was so much in the basin that they didn't have to worry that they might eat it all.

When everyone had eaten as much of the stew as they wanted, the slaves took away the basins and brought in trays of wild figs. After that the slave woman again held a bowl of water on her knee for Agebeye and the senior wife to wash their hands.

Agebeye said a prayer of thanks for the meal. The men said, "*Kada.*" And the women said, "*Bukpe.*"

Then the man slave opened the door and everyone went out into the courtyard.

The moon was shining. One of Agebeye's brothers started to strum on a three-cornered harp.

"That's called an akpata," Atuke

whispered to Cindy and Jack. "He's going to tell stories!"

Everybody seemed excited. People rushed back into the dining room to get mats to spread on the ground.

Uzi managed to find two mats. "Elonmo and I will use one," he told Atuke. "You can share the other with Cindy and Jack."

"Storytelling is a treat that's only allowed after dark," Atuke said.

Agebeye's brother told an exciting story about a prince who had to fight

with a wicked sorcerer to win a beautiful princess. Then everybody sang songs, and even the children joined in the dancing.

The stories ended when the moon went down. After that every one of Agebeye's children came to say good night to Cindy and Jack and their friends as well as to all the other grown-ups in the compound.

Agebeye took his guests into the big house where he had his own living quarters. They were given sleeping mats set in hollows against the wall.

Nobody got undressed, so Jack and Cindy didn't even take off their shoes. They were so tired that they fell asleep as soon as they lay down.

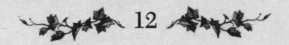

12

WHEN the first gray light of morning came through the open roof of the house, everybody began to get up.

Cindy and Jack rolled off their sleeping mats. Through the open door they saw a number of young people in the courtyard. Some held hoes. Others had big knives like the one Uzi carried.

Cindy was still rubbing the sleep from her eyes when the children in the compound came, one after the other, to wish the visitors good morning.

A little boy began to show his younger brother how to pick the seeds out of the cotton piled in a big basket.

Their older sister sat on the ground next to them and twisted the cotton into thread with a spindle.

In the middle of the room Agebeye's two sisters were weaving a long piece of cloth on a flat rack.

"Come with me, Your Highnesses." Atuke led Jack and Cindy to where Elonmo and Uzi were waiting. They all went over to say good-bye to Agebeye and his senior wife and thank them for their hospitality.

Then Agebeye joined the farm workers in the courtyard. The senior wife rushed to help soothe a crying baby.

The bongo was right where they had left it in the courtyard. It was still roped to the two poles.

Elonmo lifted one end of a pole. "Your turn now, Jack."

Jack picked up the front of the other pole. Uzi and Atuke took the rear ends, just as they had before. Cindy carried the spear and the bow and arrows.

The door to the stockade was open. Agebeye and his farmworkers waited for their guests to leave before they went to the fields.

"Head for that narrow part of the river." Elonmo pointed to a place they hadn't reached yesterday. "If we walk fast, we'll reach it before the sun comes up."

Cindy saw that there were pink streaks in the sky. She walked as fast as she could with her heavy load.

As they came closer to the river, the ground began to be sandy instead of marshy. There were tall clumps of reeds growing near the water's edge.

Before they reached the reeds, Elonmo said, "Let's put down the bongo."

The other bongo bearers were glad to do as he said.

"Now, play that song of yours," Elonmo told the jester. "I'm not in the mood for yelling."

Atuke pulled out his flute and began to play the sad sweet tune.

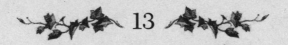

13

As soon as the music ended, there was a rustling in the reeds. Cindy wondered if a crocodile would jump out.

Instead a man with broad shoulders and powerful arms came walking around the big clump of reeds. He held out his hand. "My friend, the hunter! Can I take you across the river?"

Elonmo shook the man's hand. "Yes, I'm glad you and your ferry are still here. We're in a hurry. Back to work, you guys."

Atuke put away his flute and helped the others carry the bongo to the other side of the reeds.

Now Jack and Cindy saw the

ferryboat pulled up on the beach. It was a raft of heavy logs roped together.

A strong rope was tied to one of the strange twisted trees that grew on the riverbank. The rope stretched across the river and was tied to another tree on the opposite bank.

The ferryman helped Elonmo and the others put the bongo on the raft. Then they all pushed the raft into the water. The ferryman jumped onto it. He grabbed the rope to keep the raft from drifting away. "All aboard!"

Jack made a broad jump and landed on the raft.

Elonmo took the spear and the bow and arrows from Cindy. Uzi picked her up and waded out to the raft.

Elonmo held the weapons high over his head and stepped into the river.

Cindy was looking at the water. "There's a crocodile down there!"

Atuke took out his flute again and started to play.

The crocodile closed its eyes and seemed to smile.

Elonmo waded past it to the raft.

Then Atuke put away the ivory flute and jumped just as well as Jack had.

The sun was up now. It blazed down and glittered on the water.

A strong breeze was blowing. They all held onto the rope that stretched across the river. Together they pulled the raft to the other side.

When they reached the bank they found a group of women sitting in the shade of the tree to which the rope was tied. The women were waiting for the ferry. And they were all carrying things they had bought at the Erva fair.

After Elonmo and the others had taken the bongo ashore, they helped the women board the raft with their bundles. Then Elonmo paid the ferryman with cowry shells from a leather pouch he wore at his waist.

They watched as the ferryman and the women pulled the raft back the way it had come.

Elonmo looked at the sun. "It's getting late. Let's head for Erva."

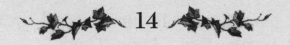

14

THE way to Erva led through deep woods, but the path was traveled so much that it was much wider than the footpath they had taken the day before. Underfoot the earth was pounded hard. Here they could use both poles to carry the bongo.

Tall forest trees arched over their heads. It seemed to Cindy and Jack that they were going through a green tunnel.

Sunlight sifted through the leaves to make bright patches on the path.

The five friends came to a group of women and children walking along.

Elonmo greeted them. The mothers smiled and moved their little ones to the side of the path so the bongo bearers could squeeze past.

59

Some time later Jack stared up at a tall palm tree. "Look, Cindy!"

"Coconuts!" Cindy remembered that they hadn't had breakfast.

"Why don't we stop for a while?" Atuke said.

"I'll climb the tree and get some coconuts," Uzi offered.

"I think we should keep going," Elonmo told them.

They marched away from the coconuts and on through the forest.

After a while Cindy saw a blaze of light at the end of the tunnel. She began to walk faster.

They stepped out of the forest into a large clearing. It was right next to a village.

Shade trees had been planted here and there. Under them groups of men and women bargained over the things they had brought to market to sell.

"This is Erva." Elonmo led them to a place in the shade where they put down the bongo.

Atuke bought chunks of coconut and wooden cups of coconut milk for all five from a woman who had set up a stand under a tree. Then he took out his flute and began to play. The people came from all over the clearing to listen.

When the jester put away his flute, he went with Jack and Cindy to see the things for sale.

There were bundles of firewood, parrots, live dogs, bags of large beans, big greenish bananas, woven cloth, straw mats, wooden cups and dishes, pepper in pods, palm oil, thread spun from cotton, dried lizards, and beautiful wood carvings.

Elonmo bought five large yams from a man who was roasting them in a charcoal fire. He tied the yams to the bongo poles.

Then Elonmo picked up the end of the pole he'd carried. Jack, Uzi, and Atuke picked up their share of the load. Cindy walked beside Elonmo as he led them through the market and past the village.

On the other side they came to a narrow dirt road.

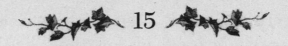

15

THERE were many travelers on the road through the forest. But nobody had a car with wheels. Four strong men came along carrying a box set on two long poles. A man sat in the box under an awning and fanned himself.

"Bow your heads!" Elonmo said in a low voice. He made a sign to everyone to move over to the side of the road to let the men and the box pass.

When they were out of sight, Jack asked, "Was that the Oba?"

Atuke laughed. "The Oba stays in his palace. Perhaps once or twice a year he comes out to perform ceremonies for the well-being of the country. The man who just went by was only a noble. He was probably going to the market."

They passed a long line of men carrying heavy loads on their heads. They were headed back the way the five friends had come.

"Is the market always this busy?" Cindy wanted to know.

"Market Day is only once a week," Atuke told her. "At Erva it's on Okuo."

"Okuo," Jack repeated. "At home it must be Tuesday. What do you call the other days of the week?"

"Eken, Orie, and Aho. There are four days in the week. They are named after the four corners of the earth." Atuke held onto his pole with one hand and pointed to the east, west, south, and north.

They rounded a bend in the road and came to a river. A bridge had been made by slinging ropes from one bank to the other and tying a walkway

of wood slats over the ropes. A rope went across the river above the walkway and served as a railing.

People were holding onto their bundles with one hand and grabbing the rope railing with the other. The bridge was as wide as the dirt road, but it swayed in the air high over the river.

High places made Cindy dizzy.

"Cindy," Jack said. "I think I see a hippopotamus down there."

Cindy decided not to look down. She held the spear and the bow and arrows with one hand and grabbed the rope railing with the other. Then she took a deep breath and stepped onto the bridge.

It gave a sickening bounce.

Cindy looked at the bank on the

other side and began to take one step at a time. It helped to pretend she was dancing. She felt a drop of water on her nose. Then another. In a minute it was raining hard.

All of a sudden Cindy remembered a man dancing in the rain in an old movie she had seen on television. She began to sing, "I'm singing in the rain! Singing in the rain! What a wonderful feeling, I'm happy again!"

The rain beat down on her head. And the bridge bounced and swayed under her feet. But by the time she stepped off the rope bridge onto the other bank, Cindy really was happy.

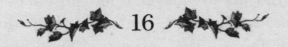

16

I⊤ rained on and off for several hours. Jack and Cindy and their friends were a bit sheltered by the leaves arching over the forest road, but after a while they began to feel damp. Still, the air was warm. They kept carrying the bongo along the road.

When the rain stopped, a wind shook the leaves of the trees and blew away the clouds. Once again the sun was blazing. Steam rose from the wet forest.

"Let's rest here," Elonmo said. Everybody thought this was a great idea.

They sat near a little tree growing in the woods not far from the road and ate the roasted yams Elonmo had bought at the market. Then they picked wild figs off the little tree for dessert.

After lunch they took to the road again. It became more and more crowded with people as they came closer to the city.

"There are nine gates to the city," Atuke told them. "This road leads to one of them."

Before they came to the gates they had to cross two moats. Each moat had a bridge of wooden planks guarded by soldiers. The soldiers looked at the tribal marks on the faces of the people before they let them cross the moats. They saw the marks on Atuke, Uzi, and Elonmo and didn't bother with the children.

The city was protected by a ten-foot-high double stockade of big trees. The gates were solid wood doors turning on a peg. Each gate was guarded by two soldiers.

"They close the gates at sundown and don't open them till daybreak," Elonmo said.

"Was that why we had to keep walking?" Cindy asked him.

The hunter nodded.

The soldiers knew Elonmo well and let them all go through the gateway into the city of Edo.

Jack and Cindy saw many wide straight streets lined with trees. There were courtyards along the streets.

Each courtyard was surrounded by a thick wall of red clay decorated with patterns pressed into the clay. Some of the walls had handsome gables and steps. In each courtyard were a number of large houses with walls of red clay polished until they looked like marble. The roofs were thatched with pressed palm leaves.

"These are the houses of the nobility," Atuke said. "A common man may not build a house with its gate along the public road, except in the courtyard of a titled chief. But come along, I want you to see the *palace*."

17

THE royal palace was built on high ground. It had a view of the river valley and the hill beyond it. The palace was half a mile across the front and a quarter of a mile from front to back.

Three golden eagles perched above twisting golden snakes on the pointed gables of the roof. Jack and Cindy saw beautiful sculptures of kings and soldiers carved into the red clay columns on each side of the tall outer doorway of the enormous palace.

Two soldiers wearing brass helmets and holding short swords were guarding the doorway. They greeted Elonmo and Atuke like old friends.

Elonmo put down his pole. The others were happy to do the same.

"We had the luck to kill this bongo yesterday," Elonmo told the soldiers. "We were hunting alone and had no bearers, so we carried it back ourselves for His Majesty. Please have someone take it to the kitchen and prepare it for the royal table."

One of the soldiers clapped his hands four times. At once four strong men came for the bongo.

"We have to say good-bye to Elonmo and Uzi now," Atuke told the children. "Huntsmen do not live in the palace."

Elonmo bowed low to Jack and held out both hands.

Jack remembered that he was supposed to give only one in return. "I hope we meet again."

Then Elonmo said good-bye to

Cindy. Oh, she thought, maybe I'll never see him anymore. "Thank you for everything!" she whispered.

When it was Uzi's turn to go, Cindy had to blink to keep the tears from her eyes.

Elonmo and Uzi said good-bye to Atuke and walked away from the palace.

The soldiers were staring at the brass rivets on Jack's jeans and the flowery print on Cindy's dress.

First one soldier and then the other bowed. They stepped aside to let Atuke and the two children go through the gateway into the palace courtyard.

Atuke took them to a well where all three washed their hands and faces. Then they walked through many gateways and large beautiful rooms. The red clay floors were polished till they shone. Little white cowry shells had been pressed into them to make handsome designs. The smooth red walls rose in seven stages to a height of over eleven feet.

Cindy and Jack walked past rooms of busy workers. They saw a brass smith casting a mask in one room. Next door carvers and carpenters were making everything from kola nut boxes to figures of gods and animals.

There were fan and leather box makers. An old man was cutting a battle scene into an ivory tusk. Musicians practiced on flutes and harps and drums. Others were making up ballads.

"All these people live in the palace," Atuke said. "Only the Oba has the right to use their work."

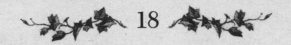 18

J ACK saw a group of men who seemed to be doing nothing. They all had bundles on their heads. "Who are those guys, Atuke?"

"Those are the Royal Carriers. They are not allowed to see the Oba without a load on their heads," the jester said.

"Really?" Cindy asked. Cindy couldn't help laughing.

Atuke looked at her. Then he grinned. "You're right. It *is* funny!"

A fat man with his head shaved except for a tuft on top frowned at Atuke. He wore a heavy necklace and a long skirt shaped like a bell. "Where have you been, Joker? The Oba has been asking for you. You'd better get over to see him at once!"

Atuke bowed. "I thank you, Obilo, for telling me that His Majesty wishes to see me. I will go at once." He looked at the children. "Their Highnesses will come with me."

Atuke led Jack and Cindy through long halls and many rooms.

Slaves were starting to light the lamps hanging on chains from the ceiling. Some lamps had a little brass bird on their chains. The birds seemed to be flying right over the flame.

The jester stopped before a carved wooden door and bowed to a man wearing a striped skirt and a necklace of colored beads. "Please tell His Majesty that I have with me a prince and princess from a far country."

The man went into the room and

came out almost at once. "You have permission to enter," he said. He bowed to Jack and Cindy, but not to Atuke.

The Oba sat on a low, square-shaped stool carved from a single block of wood. A slave was fanning him with a round leather fan.

His Majesty was not a tall man, but he looked every inch a king. His skirt was four layers of different types of cloth, each shorter than the next. He had strings of coral beads around his thin ankles and carved ivory bracelets on his arms. His high collar of coral beads reached from his shoulders to his mouth.

Colored beads were twisted into the many little braids of his hair. The crown he wore today was a round brass cap studded with coral. He was holding a strange-shaped sword.

The Oba waved a delicate-looking hand. The slave left the room and closed the door behind him.

His Majesty stood up with difficulty, tucked the sword under his arm, and held out his hand first to Jack and then to Cindy. They gave him both hands in return.

The Oba turned to Atuke. "I missed you. You've been gone a whole week!"

Both Cindy and Jack remembered that a week was only four days here.

"I went with your chief huntsman and his helper," Atuke told him. "We brought back a large bongo for Your Majesty's dinner."

"Very good," the Oba said. "When it is ready, we will all eat together. And while we are waiting, I would like to know more about the prince and princess."

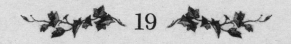

THE Oba sat down again while Jack and Cindy took turns telling how they went to the museum with their parents and found themselves in the tree in the jungle.

After they had finished, His Majesty was very quiet. He seemed to be thinking hard. At last he spoke. "Your customs are different from ours."

Atuke laughed. "They only have one wife at a time," he told the Oba.

His Majesty didn't think this was funny. "I have a hundred and seventeen wives."

"A hundred and eighteen," Atuke corrected him. "Last week the Head Chief of Utesi made you a present of his oldest daughter."

"I wish I had only one," the Oba said. "I have so many children I can't remember their names, and I haven't seen my oldest son, the Oko, since he was nine years old."

"That's terrible, Your Majesty," Jack said.

"It's not safe for the Oko to live here with all his brothers and their jealous mothers," Atuke explained. "He is guarded by a great chief until he is old enough to have his own house."

The Oba looked sad. "Many people would like to be Oba. And someone must care for the people so that there is peace and plenty. But there are customs here that I would change if I could." He looked at Cindy. "In your country," he said, "are two babies ever born at the same time to the same mother?"

"You mean twins," Cindy said. "Our neighbors have three-year-old twins."

Jack grinned. "They look just like each other. To tell which is which I hold up a mirror and say, 'Who's that?' If it's David, he says 'Gabriel' and if it's Gabriel, he says 'David.'"

Both Jack and Cindy thought this was very funny, but Atuke didn't laugh.

"Here," the jester told them, "twins are thought not to be human. They are like the litter of an animal. And they are destroyed when they are born."

"Can't their mother save them?" Cindy asked.

"She is sent away to live alone," Atuke said. "People think the gods have cursed her."

"That's terrible!" Jack said.

"One mother saved her babies," the Oba said. "I will tell you the story. Please be seated."

Atuke and the children sat on mats on the floor.

"A noble lady gave birth to a son," the Oba began. "Her ladies in waiting took the baby to be washed and dressed in fine clothing. One young woman stayed with the new mother.

"Suddenly another son was born. The young woman wrapped him in a mat from the floor so that his cries would not be heard. She slipped out of the house and took the baby to a hut in the forest. There she told people it was her child."

"Did his real mother ever see him again?" Jack asked.

"When he was four years old, the young woman took him back with her to live in the big house. He played with his twin and they became best friends. When they were grown, their mother told them that they were brothers. She warned them never to let anyone else know."

"I like that story," Cindy said.

There was a tap on the door. Atuke went to open it.

A gentleman-in-waiting came in. He bowed to the Oba. "Dinner will be served in Your Majesty's private dining room."

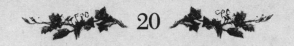 20

THE Oba led the way to his private dining room. He walked slowly as if each step was painful. Atuke followed with Cindy and Jack.

"His Majesty's senior wife is known as the *Enahan*," the jester told them. "You will like her."

The royal lady was waiting for them. She was not as young as the other women they had seen in the palace. Her hair was braided into a wreath on top of her head. She had a sweet face, but she looked tired. She smiled at the children. "I was hoping I would have a chance to meet Your Highnesses. Everyone is talking about you. You are not like anyone they have ever seen."

"Wait till you hear their story, my dear," His Majesty said.

A slave entered with a bowl of water and held it on his knee for the Oba and the Enahan to wash their hands.

Next a noble carried in a wooden box shaped like a ram's head. The Oba opened it and took out a kola nut, which he handed to Jack.

Jack repeated what he could remember of Elonmo's prayer. He broke the nut and ate a little piece. Then he gave a piece to the Oba and the others.

The noble took the ram's head box out of the room.

Gentlemen-in-waiting filled pottery cups with fresh water or palm wine. Platters of food were placed on the floor in front of the mats on which the Oba and Enahan and their guests were seated.

After that the gentlemen-in-waiting went out of the room and closed the carved wooden door behind them.

"Among the nobility, eating is a very private business!" Atuke explained to the children.

They all enjoyed the roast leg of bongo with yams and hearts of palm. There was a kind of flat bread baked from cassava root flour. For dessert they used ivory spoons with carved birds on the handles to eat stewed fruit from shiny pottery bowls.

"Now," the Oba said to Cindy, "tell the Enahan how you came to be in our country."

It took longer to tell the story this time because the Enahan kept asking questions. She even wanted to know why Cindy and Jack had clothing on their legs and feet and what a diorama was like.

At last the Oba said, "That's enough questions, my dear. Just listen to the story. At this rate, we'll be here all night. And there are some questions I want to ask *you*."

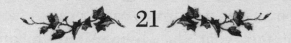

THE Enahan bowed. "What is it you wish to know, Your Majesty?"

"Are those two junior wives still quarreling?" the Oba asked.

"Yes," the Enahan told him. "Onyan and Iranele seem to hate each other." She turned to the children. "It is my duty to teach members of the court proper manners and customs. Some of these bush chieftans' daughters have no manners at all."

"Poor things," His Majesty sighed. "They thought being married to the Oba would make them important, but instead they leave the green forest to be shut up in these fancy walls with a lot of women just as important as they are. Try moving these two into apartments far from each other. Now tell me what the diviners are talking about."

The Enahan looked very sad. "It's the same old complaint."

"You mean they're tired of pigs' and goats' blood." The Oba's voice was bitter. "Now they want to sacrifice people again!"

"The chief diviner says that you are dying because the gods want human blood," the Enahan said.

"There is one god higher than the others, the Almighty God," the Oba reminded her. "He is known to be wise and kind and has never demanded human sacrifice. It is all these other gods set up as go-betweens who are said to ask for blood. I have thought long and hard about this. That is why we have had no human sacrifice in our land since I have been Oba."

"What are they talking about, Jack?" Cindy whispered.

"*Sh-sh!*" Jack put a finger to his lips.

The Oba was talking again. "It's true that I have not been well. The pots of magic charms that the doctors put at the door of my chamber have not cured me. I seem a little weaker each day." He thought a minute. "If I die, all my slaves and even Atuke will be killed so that I have servants in the next world."

"That's awful!" Cindy gasped.

"My mother would know what to do," the Oba told the children. "She is old and wise, but I am not allowed to see her now that I am Oba. The

91

Queen Mother has to live in her own palace outside the city."

The Enahan looked at Jack and Cindy. "Will the two of you go to the Queen Mother tomorrow? Tell her that the Oba is sick and ask her if I should go ahead with the plan she and I made long ago."

"Of course we'll go," Jack said. "Can Atuke come with us?"

"No. Atuke is needed here," the Enahan said. "You will have soldiers with you to see that you arrive safely. It is getting late. Come with me."

The Enahan took them to her own apartment and gave them a room with two sleeping mats covered with coarse cloth. The roof was open to the stars.

Cindy and Jack were so tired they shut their eyes and went right off to sleep.

IN the morning a slave woman woke
the children. She brought a wooden
bowl of water for them to wash in and
combed their hair with a wooden
comb.

The slave took away the water bowl
and brought them a big pottery bowl
of soup and two pretty shells for
spoons.

While they ate the soup Cindy
said, "Jack, maybe these people think
the way we wear our hair is weird."

Jack laughed. "They're pretty weird themselves. One woman has half her hair dyed red. Some others seem to be using an oil that turns their hair yellow or green."

"I saw women with a lot of little braids," Cindy said, "just like some ladies at home. But others shave the top of their heads and leave clumps of hair on each side."

"The lords and ladies seem to twist all sorts of jewelry and beads into their braids," Jack told her. "I guess that's to show that they're noble."

Cindy nodded. "Ordinary people like Atuke and Elonmo leave their hair like a great big bush." She put down her spoon and reminded her brother not to finish all the soup.

"It's really good," Jack said. "I think they put coconut in it." He stopped eating.

The Enahan came into the room. "Good morning, Your Highnesses. I hope you slept well." She looked around to be sure no one else was around. Then she handed Cindy a small ivory carving.

Cindy saw that it was the head of a young man. He wore a strange cap and had a smile on his face.

"Keep that hidden," the Enahan said.

Cindy put the carving into her pocket.

"Give it to the Queen Mother," the Enahan told her. "Say that I must have her answer as soon as possible. There is no time to lose!"

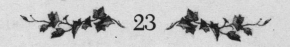

23

OUTSIDE the main gate of the palace two soldiers waited beside a large box with fancy designs cut into it. The box was set on two long poles. One little horse was harnessed between the poles at the front of the box and another one between the poles at the rear. A fringed canopy shaded the box from the burning sun.

Each soldier carried two small swords and wore a side-wrapped skirt decorated with tassels and bells. The soldiers opened a gate in the side of the box. They took out a stool that Cindy and Jack used to climb into the box. The stool was put back inside and the gate closed. Then they started on their journey to the Queen Mother's palace.

Since there weren't any wheels to bump up and down, it was like riding in a hammock.

As they rode through the city, everyone bowed and moved out of their way. When they came to the double stockade the soldiers guarding the gate opened it wide to let them go through. The little horses trotted over the bridges crossing the two moats. On either side of the box the soldiers marched with their bells jingling.

It made Jack and Cindy feel as if they really were royalty.

The Queen Mother's palace was reached by a different road than they had been on yesterday.

This palace was in a grove of trees, surrounded by a high wall of heavy logs plastered with red clay molded into the shapes of people and animals.

The guards at the outer gate knew the soldiers and the fancy box. They let them pass through.

The little horses also seemed to know where they were. They neighed and tossed their heads. Then they trotted along the tree-lined avenue to the main gate of the palace.

"We have a message for the Queen Mother from the Enahan," Cindy told the man at the head of the palace steps.

"Come inside." He led them through a courtyard and into a long low building with polished floors and many altars. He whispered something to a woman wearing a long blue skirt.

"Please wait here." The woman bowed to the children and left the room. She returned almost at once and led them into a room where a tall woman was sitting on a carved wooden stool.

She was dressed in several layers of patterned cloth and wore many gold bracelets. Her white hair was combed up into a tall point.

"This is Her Majesty, the Queen Mother," the woman in the blue skirt said.

Jack and Cindy bowed.

Her Majesty waved her hand. The woman in the blue skirt went out of the room and closed the door behind her.

24

CINDY looked up into the kind eyes of the Queen Mother. "The Enahan asked me to tell you that the Oba is very sick. She wants to know if she should go ahead with the plan you once made with her. She told me to give you this." Cindy pulled the ivory carving of the smiling man's head from her pocket.

The Queen Mother took the carving to a shrine in a corner of the room. She placed the little ivory head on the altar and knelt before it.

"Cindy," Jack said. "You forgot to tell the Queen Mother that the Enahan wants her to send an answer at once. We'll have to rush back."

Cindy opened her mouth to tell the Queen Mother this. But the Queen Mother turned away and clapped her hands. The woman in the blue skirt stepped into the room. "Send me the master of the Agba," Her Majesty commanded. The woman left the room. A few minutes later a powerful man entered.

The Queen Mother made a sign. The man bowed and went out.

"The soldiers who brought you here are tired," the Queen Mother told the children. "And so are the horses. Stay and rest a while. You can go back when the sun is not so high in the sky."

"Jack and I don't need the horses

and men. We can go back by ourselves." Cindy remembered that if the Oba died, all of his slaves and even his jester would be sacrificed. Tears came into her eyes. "I'm afraid for Atuke."

"So am I," Jack told the Queen Mother. "We have to let the Enahan know your answer to her question."

Her Majesty held up her hand. "Listen!"

Jack and Cindy heard the booming of a drum beating out a message.

The Queen Mother left the shrine and walked over to the two children. She whispered, "The Enahan *already* knows my answer."

"Your Majesty," Cindy asked, "who is the little smiling statue meant to be?"

"That is a carving of Esu, the Divine Trickster," the Queen Mother told her. "Esu may fool the diviners."

"Aren't the diviners the ones who think they have to sacrifice people because the Oba is sick?" Jack said.

The Queen Mother put her finger to her lips. "Now you must tell me who you are and how you and the jester became such good friends. Let us go out into my garden. You can talk while you eat the fruit from the trees there. Travelers have brought me seeds and plants from far places. There's no garden like it in all Edo."

She walked to a door in the wall of the room. Jack hurried to open it, and the Queen Mother stepped out into a garden. Cindy and Jack came after her.

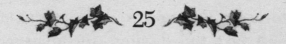

25

THE Queen Mother's garden was a little like the forests they had walked through yesterday and the day before. But here the trees were all placed where they would have just the right amount of sunshine.

There were beautiful orchids growing on the trees as well as delicious fruit of many kinds.

Jack picked two yellow bananas off a small tree with enormous leaves. He handed a banana to Cindy.

The bananas were warm and sweet and tasted much nicer than any they had ever had in Brooklyn. They ate juicy berries and several different kinds of figs.

The Queen Mother picked a round pink fruit with little lumpy sections inside. "Try this. It's my favorite." She gave the children some of the little lumps to taste.

"I've seen that in the fruit stands at home," Cindy said. "I never tasted it before. The fruit stand man told me it's called a pomegranate."

"It's time you told me your names," the Queen Mother said. "Then you can tell me about your home."

"I'm Cindy and Jack is my brother," Cindy began. She tried to explain houses with closed roofs and cars with wheels.

The Queen Mother found it hard

to believe in such things. But when Jack told her about the dioramas and how he and Cindy suddenly found themselves in a tree with the chimpanzees, she seemed to understand perfectly. "It's a simple enchantment," she told the children. "As soon as I clear up some of these other matters, I'll get to work on it and you can get back to your parents."

When they told her how they had traveled to the city with Atuke and the two huntsmen, she said, "It sounds like fun. I wish I were young enough to have gone along."

As soon as the sun was lower in the sky and a cool breeze blew through the trees, the soldiers were ready to escort the children back to the Oba's palace. The little horses were hitched to the carved box with the awning over it.

The Queen Mother said good-bye to Jack and Cindy in the garden. "Promise me," she whispered, "if you notice anything different when you return to the Oba's palace, act as if everything is just as it should be! Whatever you do, don't say *anything*, even to each other, about what you think! Promise!"

Cindy and Jack promised.

The woman in the blue skirt led the children back through the palace and out the front gate to where the soldiers and horses waited.

As soon as Cindy and Jack were safe inside the box, the horses started on their way back to the city. The soldiers marched alongside, with their swords ready for action and the bells on their tasseled skirts jingling.

26

WHEN Jack and Cindy arrived back at
the Oba's palace, the sun had begun
to set. The swinging oil lamps were
already lit in the rooms and corridors.

A gentleman-in-waiting met them
at the palace gate and took them to
where the Enahan was expecting them
in her own apartment.

After the gentleman-in-waiting had
gone out of the room and shut the
door, the Enahan made a deep bow to
the children. "Thank you," she
whispered. Aloud she said, "Your
Highnesses, His Majesty, the Oba, is
busy giving instructions to the royal
jester who is going to visit the Queen
Mother tomorrow. He begs your

pardon for not dining with you tonight. May I have the honor of your company at dinner here?"

Neither Jack nor Cindy knew how to answer. They both decided to bow.

The Enahan clapped three times and a parade of servants brought in the dinner.

During the meal the Enahan asked after the health of the Queen Mother.

"She looked healthy to me," Jack said, "but maybe she had banged her head. She had her hair twisted up into a tall point."

"That's a hairstyle called *The Fowl's Peak*," the Enahan told them. "Only a Queen Mother may wear it. If my son, the Oko, is crowned Oba, I will have the right to wear my hair like that."

Jack turned red and wished he hadn't said anything.

The Enahan smiled. "Just think

what things I might say in your country. I'd ask what was wrong with everybody's feet because they covered them!"

Jack felt better at once.

Cindy remembered that Atuke had said that she and Jack would like the Enahan. "Why is Atuke going to see the Queen Mother?" she asked.

"He is not feeling well. The Queen Mother has studied the art of medicine. The Oba is fond of his jester and wants him to have the best of care," the Enahan said. "Would you and your brother like to go with your friend? I am sure you will be welcome to stay at the Queen Mother's palace."

Cindy swallowed hard. What was the matter with Atuke? He was all right the last time she and Jack had seen him!

Jack reached over and gave her a

little pinch. She stared at him. Then she remembered what the Queen Mother had said about acting as if everything was just as it should be.

Cindy couldn't think what to say, so Jack spoke for both of them. "Atuke has been our friend," he said. "And we want to go with him to help in any way we can."

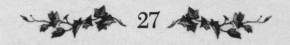

27

CINDY couldn't get to sleep for a long time. She kept thinking about Atuke. Why should he be sick? Maybe somebody in the palace had poisoned him. All the nobles seemed to hate him because the Oba liked him so much!

She longed to talk to Jack about it, but she had promised the Queen Mother not to say anything.

Next morning everybody in the palace was up before dawn. And everybody was excited.

The slave woman who brought breakfast to Cindy and Jack was beaming. "The doctors have at last cured His Majesty!" she told the children. "He is going to open the new market in town today!"

Cindy looked at Jack. His face was white. He must be thinking the same thing she was. The diviners had *sacrificed* someone to save the Oba! It would take magic to cure him so quickly!

Neither Cindy nor Jack wanted breakfast. They just pretended to eat.

As soon as they seemed to have had enough, the Enahan came for the children. She led them to the outer gate of the palace. The little horses were already hitched to the carved box, and the soldiers were waiting.

A man came walking slowly out of the big palace gate. The soldiers in the brass helmets greeted him. "We heard you weren't well, Atuke," one of them said. "I hope you will feel better soon."

The jester nodded his thanks.

Jack and Cindy stared. Something

terrible must have happened to Atuke
to make him look so weak. Maybe he
hadn't had anything to eat while they
were away! And why wasn't there a
special travel box for him, even if he
wasn't a noble?

The jester bowed to the Enahan
and the children.

"Your Majesty," Cindy said to the
Enahan. "Please let Atuke ride. Jack
and I would rather walk."

"That's why we wear clothes on our feet," Jack said.

The Enahan smiled. She reached out her hand to them. When they gave her theirs in return, she bent over and kissed them.

The soldiers opened the gate in the carved box and helped the jester into it.

Just then the fat man with the tuft of hair on top of his head came puffing out of the gate. He made a low bow to the Enahan and two more to Jack and Cindy.

"What is it, Obilo?" the Enahan asked.

"His Majesty wishes to see Their Royal Highnesses before they leave for the Queen Mother's palace," the noble told her.

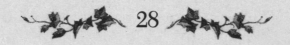

28

THE Enahan led Jack and Cindy to the carved wooden door of the room where they had first met the Oba. The man guarding the door opened it for the children.

They went inside, but the Enahan did not follow. The door was closed behind them.

Jack and Cindy had never been alone with the Oba of Edo.

He seemed to be wearing even more splendid clothes than before.

Cindy thought he looked weighted down with all those coral beads in the high collar that almost covered his mouth.

His hair looked shiny and freshly braided with gold and coral under the heavy coral crown. Besides all of this he was wearing a cape made of coral beads.

He was not sitting on the wooden stool now. Instead he was standing in the middle of the room.

Cindy thought he looked as if he'd never been sick in his life. She remembered how delicate his hands and feet had been. They seemed as strong and rough as Atuke's now.

All the coral was red and shiny in the morning sunshine coming through the open roof. It made Jack and Cindy blink. The man in the crown did not say a word. He held out his hand to each of the children in turn.

Cindy looked up. The lower part of the royal face was hidden by the royal collar, but the royal eyes looked just like Atuke's! Suddenly she had a crazy idea. What if Atuke and the Oba were twins, and the Enahan had changed their clothes and their hairdos?

Then she caught a glimpse of something tucked into the folds of the many layers of royal skirts. Cindy pulled it out.

Jack couldn't understand what she was doing. Then he saw that his sister was holding the little ivory flute Atuke always kept with him!

Cindy was about to say something.

The man in the crown put his finger to his lips.

Jack clapped his hand over Cindy's

mouth. "We'd better give this to your mother, Your Majesty. It's just one more thing to weight you down."

The man wearing the heavy crown grinned. "You're right, Jack," he said. "Atuke has been playing this flute almost all his life. He will want it when he is cured of his ailment."

He picked up the royal Sword of State. "Now I must say good-bye," he said in a loud voice. "I wish you a good journey home. Please give my love to the Queen Mother."

Suddenly he bent over and hugged both the children. Cindy was sure she saw tears in his eyes.

He clapped his hands. The door was opened, and he strode forth to open the new market in town.

29

THE Enahan was waiting outside the Oba's door. She took Cindy and Jack back to where the soldiers and horses were waiting with the carved box.

"Guard Their Royal Highnesses with your life!" the Enahan told the soldiers.

Jack and Cindy held their heads high and looked as royal as they could. They walked side by side in front of the first of the two little horses. The people in the town bowed as they went by. When they came to the gates and the bridges, the soldiers there bowed, too.

Soon they were on the road to the Queen Mother's palace. They marched at a steady pace and didn't say a word. Both of them were afraid if they talked

they might somehow betray the Oba's secret.

It was a long walk in the hot sun. When at last they reached the Queen Mother's palace, a strong slave was waiting to carry the sick passenger into the palace.

The woman in the long blue skirt stood at the gate. She bowed to the two children. "Her Majesty is waiting for you."

Cindy and Jack followed her to the Queen Mother's room. The woman went out and closed the door.

The Queen Mother was kneeling in front of the shrine. A shaft of sunlight came through the open roof onto the altar. It lit up the smile on the little ivory face of Esu, the Divine Trickster.

When she heard the door close,

the Queen Mother stood up. She tiptoed over to the children and kissed them.

Jack took the ivory flute from under his shirt. Without a word he handed it to Her Majesty.

"I gave that to Atuke when he was four years old," she said. "No one can play it as he does." She took the flute to the altar and laid it beside the ivory head of Esu. "It will be safe here until Atuke can play it again."

"Your son told me to give you his love," Jack said.

When the woman in the blue skirt came back, the Queen Mother told her, "Their Royal Highnesses are tired from their journey. Bring them something to eat and drink. I must go to the Royal Jester."

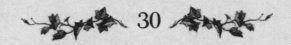

30

Jack and Cindy sat on mats and ate fruit from the Queen Mother's garden. They were still afraid to talk about what had happened. Cindy could bear it no longer and was going to say something when Her Majesty returned.

"How is Atuke?" Jack asked.

"Better already," the Queen Mother told him. "Some people can't stand being shut up behind walls. Atuke is in the garden. It reminds him of the forest he loves."

Cindy remembered that Atuke said the Oba only came out of the palace once or twice a year. "His Majesty went into the town to open a market today," she told the Queen Mother.

Her Majesty smiled. "Good for him! My son doesn't like being cooped up any more than his jester does. After Atuke recovers his health, there'll be some changes made around the Oba's palace."

The Queen Mother walked to the altar and picked up a small round tray. Four figures were carved into the wooden rim. In the center was wood dust. She lifted the lid of a bowl shaped like a hen and took out sixteen

palm nuts. She used the nuts to make a pattern in the wood dust. "This is a divining tray," she said.

Her Majesty took a carved ivory stick from the altar. "We'll need this." She walked to the door in the wall.

Jack hurried to open it for her. Then the children followed the Queen Mother into the garden.

The man they now knew to be the Oba was sitting in a swing hanging from one of the trees. He looked better already and even more like his twin brother Atuke. "There are wild animals in your garden," he told his mother.

"They come after the fruit," Her Majesty said. She placed the divining tray on the ground and knelt over it. "Each of you children must put something into the tray." She tapped it with the ivory stick.

Cindy took out her shiny penny
and dropped it into the tray.

Jack pulled the M&M's bag out of
his pocket. There was only one candy
in it.

A very small ape ran from behind
a tree and reached for the candy.

"Don't let the monkey get it!" the Oba said.

Jack dropped the M&M into the tray, and the Queen Mother tapped it again with her ivory stick.

"It's not a monkey," Jack said. "It's a chimpanzee!"

The little chimp had one arm stretched out, but it wasn't moving now. And he seemed farther away than he did a moment ago. The garden seemed different, too. Cindy and Jack couldn't see the Oba or the Queen Mother anywhere.

They looked around. Their mother and father were walking toward them.

"Come and look at the other dioramas, kids," Mr. Edwards said. "You ought to have seen enough of this one by now."